Dedicated to all of the kids out there of all ages big and small, to their wild, great, awesome and wonderful imaginations.

Order this book online at www.trafford.com
or email orders@trafford.com

Most Trafford titles are also available at major online book retailers.

Printed in the United States of America.

ISBN: 978-1-4669-4868-6 (sc)
ISBN: 978-1-4669-4869-3 (e)

Library of Congress Control Number: 2012913067

Trafford rev. 08/14/2012

 www.trafford.com

North America & international
toll-free: 1 888 232 4444 (USA & Canada)
phone: 250 383 6864 ♦ fax: 812 355 4082

Other books by JB Mounteer

Camp were wolf

Camp were wolf, is a fun filled, surprising, adventure, about a boy named Buddy, who goes to a summer camp in the mountians. The same mountians where his parents grew up. He meets a variety of new friends and learns about the legends of werewolves and vampires. There are a many twists, thrilling surprises hints of what might happen and a ending that leaves you wanting more, and knowing why you should never judge someone or something, before you truly know them.

Franky Frankinstain

Mr. and Mrs. Frankinstain, two doctors of weird and strange science, have always wanted to have children, but have never had the time. So on one dark and stormy night they decided to build one. The new little Franky Frankinstain, built of nuts, bolts and spare parts from around the lab, learns all he can from his parents and then goes to school. Join J.B. Mounteer, in this fun-filled story about making new friends, challenges at school and trying to win first place! When Franky and Charley are partnerd for the annual go-cart race, they find that math really can help them beat the notorious Bossy sisters, who will stop at nothing to win. When it comes down to the final turn, will Franky and Charley be able to win using math? Or will the Bossy sisters cheating ruin their chances for victory?

Chapter One

Jorey Jakob sat in the school cafeteria chewing on something that a lunch lady claimed was a piece of meat but tasted more like rubber—and he winced with every bite. Jorey was listening to his friends talk excitedly about their favorite thing: scary movies. It was Friday, which meant a late-night movie for these third graders.

"My dad said we should rent *Furious Mummy!*" Porto Pertmyer proclaimed through a large mouthful of green beans. Porto was one of Jorey's best friends and the largest boy in the school; he loved to eat. His friends said it was his best talent: He would eat anything at any time.

Timmy Turken, Jorey's other best friend and the smallest kid in school, slowly shook his head. "I don't think so!" he said so loudly it echoed throughout out the cafeteria. "*The Werewolves' Revenge* is the scariest movie of the year!"

Jorey choked, causing his chocolate milk to shoot out of his nose and splat an unsuspecting Mary Miller in the face. Mary grunted her disapproval, lifted her nose in the air, and left the table. Porto and Timmy giggled.

All of the boys had seen previews of *The Werewolves' Revenge*, and the previews alone had given them nightmares, especially Jorey. For as long as Jorey could remember, he had always been terrified of werewolves. He was even afraid of the word werewolf. Just thinking of it sent him running into his parents' room at night—and that's pretty embarrassing for a third grader.

Jorey shivered and drank the last of his chocolate milk. The other boys were smiling and nodding their heads. Jorey put on a fake smile and said, "Uh . . . yeah, that's supposed to be pretty scary all right."

"You bet it is!" Timmy said. "And it comes out on video today!"

"Really?" Porto shouted, shoving in another mouthful of beans. "We should rent it!"

Sharp cold chills ran through Jorey's body. "No!" he shouted, gripping the table in fear.

Timmy and Porto looked at him with confused looks. "What's the matter, Jorey?" Timmy giggled, playfully elbowing Porto. "You scared or something?"

Jorey swallowed hard and put back on his fake smile. "Me? Scared? No way!"

"Look," Porto said, patting Jorey's back. "We know you're scared, Jorey. Every time someone even says the word werewolf, you turn white as a ghost."

"That's not true!" Jorey snapped as his skin turned as white as the tablecloth.

Timmy and Porto laughed. "What if I promise to hold your hand through the whole movie?" Timmy said.

"I'm not scared!" Jorey shouted, pounding his fist on the table and turning red with anger. "And I'll prove it!" He picked up his food tray and stood up. "As soon as I get home from school today, I'll ask my dad to rent it!"

"All right!" Timmy and Porto shouted, giving each other a high five. "We'll be over at seven o'clock!"

Jorey sighed, walked over to the garbage can, and dumped his tray. What was he going to do? He really didn't want to rent that movie. He didn't want to look like a scaredy cat in front of his two best friends either.

For the rest of the day, Jorey dragged himself around school. He was determined to find a way out of this horrible situation. Maybe he could fake sick; sometimes his mom fell for that one. No, Timmy and Porto would see through that like glass. Maybe he could convince his parents to take him out of town for the weekend; his dad loved road trips. No, that wouldn't work either. This was his mom's scour-the-house weekend, and nobody messed with her cleaning—not even dad. His only hope was his dad. Dad didn't like to rent movies; he thought it a waste of time and money.

"Books," he would always say. "Now there's something to spend time and money on."

By the time school let out and Jorey made it home, he was so exhausted from worrying all day, he just dropped his backpack on the floor and fell face first on the couch. He was just about asleep when his dad shook his back.

"Are you awake, bud?" Jorey rolled over lazily to see his dad looking down at him with an enormous, toothy grin. "I've got a surprise for you! Some real good news!"

Jorey's dad was bobbing on his feet like a giddy schoolboy. Mom always said he acted like her oldest child.

Jorey dropped his head. "Right now I could use some good news."

His dad giggled, plopped himself on the couch next to Jorey, and tossed something in his lap. "This should cheer you up, bud!"

Jorey picked the object up with shaky hands, and stared at it with wide, frightened eyes.

"I know how you and your friends love to watch scary movies on Fridays." He slapped Jorey's knee playfully. "You think that one will be scary enough?"

Jorey tried to stop his knees from shaking as he read the title of the movie out loud. "*The Werewolves' Revenge.*"

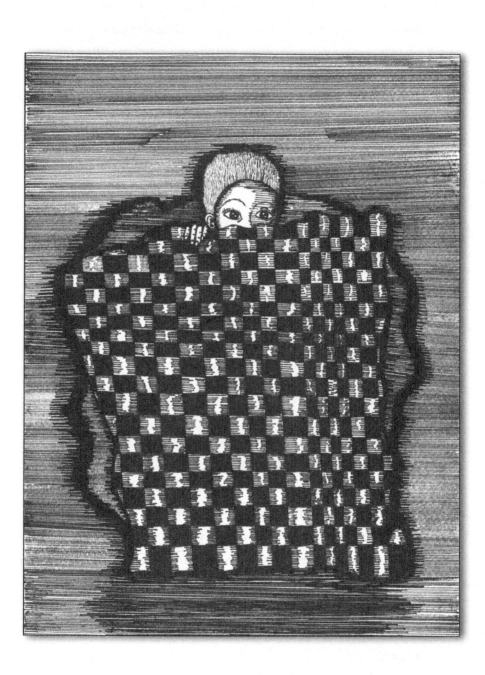

Chapter Two

By the time seven o clock rolled around, Jorey was so nervous and sweaty that he looked like he had taken a shower with his clothes on. All through dinner, he kept trying to come up with excuses for why he shouldn't have his movie party, but they were all lame.

When the doorbell rang, Jorey jumped right out of his skin. He thought about not answering the door, but he knew his mom or dad would if he didn't. He took a deep breath and then slowly started to open the door.

Before he had even opened it halfway, Porto and Timmy pushed their way through. Porto's arms were full of goodies, snacks, and a large bag of popcorn. They were both wearing goofy smiles.

"Did he get it?" Porto said through a mouthful of chips. "Did he get the movie?"

"Yeah, did he get it?" asked Timmy.

Jorey smiled back as best he could and nodded. "Yeah, he got it."

"All right!" Porto and Timmy shouted, giving each other a high five. They ran over to the giant beanbags in front of the big screen TV and dove in.

Just then, the front door opened, and in walked Jorey's older brother, Jaden. Jaden was in seventh grade and worked in the neighborhood walking dogs; he was earning money to buy a new bike. He was usually in a good mood, but he looked grumpy.

"What's wrong, Jaden?" Jorey asked.

Jaden lifted up his pant leg to show a small bite mark on a bloody heel. "Mrs. Jenkins's poodle bit me. She's the orneriest dog I've ever met!"

"Wow, Jaden! That looks like it hurts."

"Are we gone watch this movie or what?" asked Timmy as he bounced on the beanbag.

"Yeah," added Porto. "I'm almost out of food."

"What movie did you guys get?" asked Jaden.

"*The Werewolves' Revenge.*" Timmy and Porto shouted.

"That's supposed to be the scariest movie of the year," Jaden said. "I'd love to watch it with you guys, but I've got a ton of homework to do—and I have to take care of this bite." He turned and looked Jorey in the eyes. "You going to be all right?" he whispered, placing a hand on Jorey's shaking shoulder. "I know how you feel about werewolves."

Jorey nodded, and tried to put on a brave face. "I'll be fine—but would you mind if I slept in your room tonight?" he whispered.

Jaden rubbed his little brother's head and smiled. "Sure you can, buddy."

"Thanks, Jaden," Jorey whispered.

When Jorey walked over to pick up the movie, he was shaking so bad he could hardly put it in.

"Come on, scaredy-cat," said Timmy. "Put it in already!"

"You want me to do it for you?" added Porto.

Jorey finally pushed in the movie, plopped down on a beanbag, and pulled a blanket over his lap. All through the movie, Jorey kept pulling his blanket higher and higher—and his eyes kept closing tighter and tighter. By the time the movie was over, the blanket was all the way over his head, and his eyes were squeezed shut as tight as he could get them.

When he finally got up the courage to look out from his hiding place, Timmy and Porto had their arms around each other, their mouths were hanging open, and their eyes were full of fear.

"That was d-d-definitely the scariest movie I have ever seen!" Timmy said as he pulled himself out of Porto's crumb-covered arms.

"Sure was!" Porto said as he shoved the last of the popcorn in his mouth. "Do you think your d-dad could give us a ride home? I don't feel like walking tonight."

"Me neither," muttered Timmy. "That movie was too scary!"

"I'll go ask him," Jorey said, thinking how scared he would be if he had to walk home.

Chapter Three

While his dad was taking his friends home, Jorey took his blanket and crept into Jaden's room.

"Jaden," he whispered, "you still awake?"

There was a snore for an answer. Jorey looked around the room at all the creepy shadows, the dark corners, and the black hole under the bed. He swallowed hard, slid himself into a corner, and covered his head with his blanket. Jorey tried not to think about the movie, the darkness, or werewolves, but he couldn't control his mind. He tried to think about how fun it would be this weekend, he tried to think about his parents—but nothing worked. His mind always came back to werewolves.

When Jorey was finally able to fall asleep, he tossed and turned with dark dreams and nightmares full of werewolves. He dreamed that he was bitten by a werewolf—and that he was turned into one. He woke with a fright and sat straight up. He looked at the clock that was glowing red on Jaden's dresser; it was midnight. He was sweating harder than when Mr. Hardcore made them run laps around the gym in P.E. He wiped the sweat from his brow and eyes and looked slowly around the room.

It was too dark to see Jaden in his bed. He could see the glow of what he assumed was the nightlight coming from the bathroom down the hall. He stood up, waited to get his balance, and then walked toward the bathroom. As he got closer, he could hear someone humming. He slowed as he got nearer and stopped at the door to listen. The door was cracked open and the light was on inside. He could see Jaden's reflection in the mirror. He was admiring himself, looking from side to side.

Suddenly Jaden stopped, and peered closer at himself in the mirror. A smile slowly crept on his face as he rubbed his upper lip. When Jorey put his eye to the crack in the door to get a better look, his body froze with fear.

Jaden was starting to grow hair on his upper lip. Jorey couldn't believe his own eyes. He rubbed them to be sure he wasn't dreaming. He couldn't move, and he was too terrified to scream. Jaden—his own flesh and blood—was turning into a werewolf!

Jorey turned and sprinted down the hall to his parents' room. He was running so fast that he missed the turn and slammed into the bedroom wall. His breath was knocked out of him, and he landed on the floor. He was up like a flash and dove right between his parents.

"Jorey," his mom said sleepily, "what are you doing out of bed, honey? It's the middle of the night."

Jorey threw his arms around her. "There's a werewolf in our bathroom!" He sobbed into her shoulder.

She looked over to where his dad was snoring heavily, then back to Jorey. "There's no werewolf in the bathroom, honey, so why don't you go climb back in bed?"

Jorey shook his head. "No, this time there really is, Mom!" He dove under the covers.

She shook her head; his dad was still snoring.

"I knew that movie was a bad idea." She looked down to console Jorey, but he was already fast asleep, shaking and moaning from nightmares.

The next morning, Jorey was up bright and early. He wanted to be up and gone before Jaden was out of bed. He ran into his room, got dressed, and then ran back to his parents' room.

"Mom, Dad, I'm going over to Timmy's house. I'll be back before lunch."

"Okay," his dad muttered through the covers.

"Be careful, honey," his mom said.

Jorey ran back down the hall and stopped dead in his tracks in front of Jaden's room. Deep down, he wanted to run like crazy, but he just had to see how much his poor brother had changed. He slowly peeked around the corner. Jaden was yawning and stretching in bed. When he stretched his arms above his head, Jorey froze with fear. Sharp chills ran up and down his spine.

Again he couldn't believe his eyes. Not only was Jaden growing hair on his lip, he had hair growing under his arms.

Jorey bolted down the hall and out the front door. He didn't stop running until he was standing at Timmy's front door. He pounded and pounded until a drowsy, scruffy faced man opened the door.

"Jorey," said Timmy's dad. "What could you possibly want this early in the morning?"

Jorey threw his hands in the air. "I've got to talk to Timmy! It's an emergency!"

Timmy's dad scratched his balding head. "He's still asleep, but I guess you could go wake him up."

Jorey sprinted into Timmy's bedroom, and jumped on his bed. "Timmy, are you awake?"

Timmy opened his eyes and blinked sleepily at Jorey.

"What are you doing here?"

Jorey stared Timmy straight in the eyes, trying to look as focused and serious as he could.

"You've got to listen to me. I've got horrible news." He swallowed hard, trying to calm himself. "I think my brother is a werewolf."

Timmy shook his head, wiped the sleepiness from his eyes, and said, "What on earth are you talking about? And get off me!" He shoved Jorey off the bed.

Jorey pushed himself off the floor, leaned over the bed, and told Timmy everything about Jaden.

"So what do you think?"

"I think you're nuts!" Timmy pulled the blanket over his head. "I mean, how could he suddenly be a werewolf? Don't you have to be bitten or something?"

"He's got a point, you know," Porto said from under the bed.

Porto's head poked out from under the bed. He was chewing a piece of peppered jerky.

"What are you doing here?" Jorey asked.

Porto took another bite of jerky. "I was too scared to sleep at my house last night, so I stayed here with Timmy." He pulled himself out from under the bed and stood next to Jorey. "So . . . what about your brother? He didn't get bitten."

Jorey looked at them both in turn and smiled knowingly. "He did get bitten. Remember?"

Chapter Four

Timmy and Porto looked at each other with recognition in their eyes and their mouths wide open.

"The dog bite!"

Jorey nodded his head and lowered his eyebrows. "The changes all started after he was bitten by the poodle!"

"We should call the dog pound," Porto said, scratching his head with a hard candy.

Timmy gave Porto a dirty look. "He's a werewolf, not a dog!" He punched him in the shoulder.

Porto rubbed his arm. "Well . . . a werewolf is kind of a dog."

"You should tell your parents," Timmy said, patting Jorey's shoulder. "They'll know what to do."

Jorey shook his head. "They wouldn't believe me—and even if they did, they would just turn him in to some scientist for experiments or something."

"I've got a question," Porto said. "Why hasn't he changed all the way into a werewolf?"

"I've been thinking about that," Jorey said. "Timmy, do you have a calendar?"

Timmy reached into his desk drawer and pulled out a calendar. "Here you go."

"Look here." Jorey pointed at the calendar. "The full moon isn't until next week. I think he is slowly changing and will become a full-blown, evil-eyed, flesh-eating, fang-bearing, claw-wearing, ratty-haired, tick-flea-ridden werewolf next week. That gives us one week to figure out a way to help him."

The three friends brainstormed the things that they knew about werewolves, but to their surprise, it wasn't very much.

Jorey stood up and put his hands on his hips. "We have got to learn more about werewolves, or else we will never be able to help him!"

Porto jumped up, causing a bag of chips to spill onto the floor. "I know! Let's go to the library. They probably have tons of books on this sort of stuff!"

They told their parents where they were going, got on their bikes, and rode off.

When they got to the library, Jorey asked, "Do you know where you keep the books on werewolves?"

"Yeah," said Timmy with a wink. "The real ones."

The librarian smiled and pointed. "Down aisle three. Myths and legends."

The boys checked out every book they could find about werewolves, which ended up being only six.

"I sure hope we find a cure for my brother in one of these." Jorey said as they tied the books to their bikes.

Back at Jorey's house, they hid the books behind their backs so Jaden wouldn't see them. In the kitchen, Jorey's mom was cleaning under the refrigerator. Like a mechanic under a car.

"You boys have fun?"

"Yes, Mom," Jorey called as they headed down the hall toward his room.

When they were passing Jaden's room, they could hear him singing along with the radio. Jaden's voice cracked, and he let out a vicious, ear-splitting howl. They stopped dead in their tracks.

What was that?" Porto asked, almost dropping his chocolate bar.

"I think he just howled at the radio," Timmy whispered, grabbing Porto's arm.

Jorey looked at them and said, "I told you my brother is a werewolf."

Jaden's door opened and he walked out into the hallway. The three boys jumped back with fright and froze flat against the wall, trying to melt themselves into it.

"What's up with you guys?" he asked, shaking his head. "You look like you've seen a ghost."

The three boys gulped. "Uh," said Jorey. "Uh, we were just going to my room."

"What you guys going to do in there?"

They tried to push the books farther behind their backs, looked at each other, and gulped again.

"Were going to do homework." Jorey said. "Yeah, that's it—homework."

"Yeah, homework." Timmy and Porto added.

Jaden nodded. "Good idea. I was practicing for chorus, but my voice keeps cracking—I think it's changing."

"Uh," said Jorey, "we better get going."

The other boys nodded and stared at Jaden. Jaden smiled and rubbed Jorey's head, causing Jorey to flinch. Jaden asked, "What's wrong with you today?"

"We're just in a hurry to get our home work done, that's all."

"Okay." Jaden turned and started to walk away. "I'll see you guys later."

They sprinted to Jorey's room and slammed the door behind them.

"Whew!" said Porto. "That was close."

"Yeah." Timmy sat down on the bed and put his books on his lap. "What would have happened if he had caught us with these books?"

"I don't know," Jorey said, "but I do know that we have to help him. So let's get busy."

Chapter Five

After a few hours of reading, the boys sat in Jorey's bedroom contemplating what they had read.

"We learned more from the movie last night than theses books tell us!" Jorey said.

"Hey look at this!" Porto shouted. "It says here that silver will hurt werewolves."

"We don't want to hurt him," Jorey said, shaking his head. "We want to find a cure."

"Well," said Timmy, "if silver hurts him, what happens when he uses silverware to eat?"

Jorey shot to his feet with a look of terror. "We've got to get to the kitchen and hide all the silverware!" He bolted to the kitchen—and Timmy and Porto hurried after.

In the kitchen, Jorey's mom was cooking lunch. "Are you boys hungry?"

"Uh, sure," Jorey said, walking toward his mother. He put his hands behind his back so Timmy and Porto could see them, and pointed toward the silverware drawer.

Timmy and Porto tiptoed over—and quickly put all the silverware in their pockets. When they were done, they ran back to Jorey's room.

Jorey started to follow them, but his mom stopped him. "I thought you guys were hungry?"

"I guess we can wait until dinner," he said, and ran to his room.

When Jorey got to his room, Timmy and Porto were shoving the silverware under his bed.

"Good job, guys. My mom didn't see a thing."

"You owe us for that one," Timmy said, rubbing his behind. "The forks in my back pocket kept poking me. I bet I have four holes in my backside."

"Me too," Porto said, reaching into his pocket, "and they smashed my gummy worms too!

"Well at least we saved Jaden from the silver," Jorey said. "But we still haven't found a way to stop him from changing."

"I've got an idea," Porto said as he filled his mouth with gummy worms. "When he falls asleep, we could shave his face and armpits."

"That's a crazy idea," Timmy said.

Jorey stood up and smiled a sinister smile. "Yeah, so crazy it just might work! Call your parents and see if you can stay the night—and I'll go get what we need!"

While Timmy and Porto called their parents, Jorey grabbed his dad's shaving cream and razor from the bathroom. Within moments, they all met back in Jorey's room.

"Can you guys stay?" Jorey hid the razor and shaving cream under his pillow.

"Yeah," said Timmy. "We both can."

"All right!" Jorey said. "Okay, here's what we'll do. First we'll shave his upper lip because that's the most noticeable. If my parents see hair there, they'll know he's changing. Second, we'll shave his armpits—that's going to be the hard part."

"Why is that the hard part?" Porto asked.

"Because we have to lift his arms and keep him asleep at the same time."

When Jorey's mom called them for dinner, they were so hungry that they ran to the kitchen.

His mom was scratching her head in wonder.

"I'm sorry, boys," she said, looking around the kitchen, "but I can't seem to find the silverware." She opened a drawer to have one last look. "I guess we'll have to use plastic."

"That's okay, Mom," Jaden said. "I don't mind eating off plastic."

Timmy leaned close to Jorey and whispered, "That's because he knows silver will hurt him."

The friends raced each other to the table, none of them wanted to have the chair next to a werewolf. In the end, Jorey lost.

As Jaden sat down, he ruffled Jorey's hair, causing Jorey to flinch.

"Did you guys finish your homework?"

"Homework?" Jorey asked. "Oh yeah . . . homework. It might take all night, so Timmy and Porto are going to spend the night."

"Oh really?" Jaden said, looking at Timmy and Porto. "That will be fun."

Both boys gulped; neither of them liked the thought of spending the night in the same house as a werewolf.

All through dinner, the three boys stared at Jaden. When they went back to Jorey's room, Timmy asked, "Did you guys see the way Jaden scarfed down that meat? He's definitely a werewolf."

"Well Porto was worse." Jorey said. Porto was rubbing his belly with a satisfied smile.

"Yeah, and I'm not a werewolf—and I always eat that way."

"I've got a question," Timmy said. "How are we supposed to keep Jaden from waking up and finding us shaving his face?"

"Well," said Jorey. "We had turkey for dinner and that always puts Jaden and my dad into an undisturbable, unwakeable, unmovable deep sleep."

Suddenly a loud snore escaped from Porto on the floor. He was rubbing his plump belly, sleeping soundly as a baby bear. "I guess it puts Porto out too."

"Well," said Timmy. "It looks like it's up to just you and me."

Jorey agreed. He reached under his pillow and pulled out the shaving cream and battery-powered razor. Jorey flipped on the switch, but Jorey quickly shut it off.

"That's kind of loud," Timmy said. "Don't you think that noise will wake him up?"

"You're right, but I think I've got something to help."

He walked over to his messy closet, and started rummaging through it. "I found them." He handed a pair of earmuffs to Timmy. "These should help—don't you think?"

Timmy studied the earmuffs for a moment, and then placed them over his ears. "Okay. Turn it on and I'll see if I can hear it."

Jorey flipped on the switch and asked, "Can you hear it?"

"What? I can't hear you!"

Jorey shut off the razor. "Take off the earmuffs!"

"What did you say?"

"I can't hear you—let me take off the earmuffs." He took them off and handed them to Jorey.

"Them things work great—I couldn't hear you or the razor."

Jorey smiled as he took them off. "All right. Now we just have to wait until everybody falls asleep."

Chapter Six

The boys spent the next two hours playing video games and talking about the mission. They still had *The Werewolves' Revenge*, but neither of them felt much like watching it. Finally they saw Jaden go into his bedroom.

"Will he go right to sleep?" asked Timmy, peeking out Jorey's door.

"Sometimes he reads before bed, but I don't think he will tonight. He looked pretty tired."

Timmy put his ear to the wall that connected their rooms.

"What are you doing?" asked Jorey.

Timmy smiled like a detective plotting a case. "I'm listening."

Jorey walked over and put his ear to the wall. "I can hear him walking around."

"Right! And when we hear him snore, we know he's asleep."

"Good thinking."

It wasn't long before they heard Jaden snoring.

"Are you ready?" Jorey asked, picking up the shaving cream and razor.

Timmy picked up the earmuffs. "Ready."

They stepped over Porto and tiptoed down to Jaden's door.

"Oh, no!" Jorey whispered.

"What's wrong?"

"The door is closed."

"Can't you just open it?"

"It's a really squeaky door, but I'll try to do it slowly."

The door squeaked. Jaden stop snoring for a second, but then he started again even louder.

"That was close," Jorey whispered. "Hey! I can't see where Jaden is."

"I can't see anything either. What are we going to do?"

"I guess we will just have to feel our way." The boys felt their way along the wall until they bumped into Jaden's bed. "We're here. I'll feel my way to his head—and then you hand me the earmuffs."

"Ooof!" Timmy gasped.

"Shush! What are you doing?"

"Sorry. I stubbed my toe."

Jorey worked his way to the top of the bed. "I found his head. Hand me the earmuffs."

Timmy handed the earmuffs to Jorey, and Jorey carefully placed them over Jaden's ears. Jaden moved a little but stayed asleep.

"I found his lips," Jorey whispered. "Hand me the shaving cream."

"Are you sure you're supposed to use shaving cream with an electric razor?"

"How am I supposed to know? I've never shaved before!"

Timmy handed the can of shaving cream to Jorey. Jorey shook it a few times, like he had seen his dad do, and then sprayed some on Jaden's upper lips.

"Oh, no!"

"What's wrong?" said Timmy. "I can't see. What's going on?"

"I can't shut off the shaving cream," Jorey said. "It's spraying all over his face!"

Jaden let out a loud snort, blasting shaving cream all over them. Then he started moving around.

"Go! Go!" Jorey pushed Timmy toward the door. "Hurry! Jaden's waking up!" They scrambled back to the door and sprinted down the hall to Jorey's room. "Hurry!" he said, jumping into bed. "Pretend you're asleep!"

Timmy threw himself on the floor, and pretended to snore. They could hear Jaden stumbling down the hall, stomping, kicking, and saying naughty words. Holding as still as they could, except for an occasional fake snore, they waited until Jaden had gone to the bathroom, washed his face, and returned to his room.

After what seemed like an eternity, Jorey asked, "Timmy, are you awake?"

"Yeah. Do you think he knows it was us?"

"I don't think so. Sometimes he does strange things when he sleepwalks. He probably just thinks this is one of those times." He paused for a moment. "At least I hope he does."

Chapter Seven

They stayed up late, talking about their failed mission, how they almost had gotten caught, and what to do next.

"Garlic," Timmy said eagerly. "We should give him garlic."

"I thought garlic was for vampires."

"Well," Timmy said as he rolled over in his blanket on the floor, "it might work on werewolves too—unless you have a better idea."

Jorey shook his head and pulled up his covers. "No, I don't. I guess we could dump some garlic on his eggs in the morning and see what happens."

"All right," Timmy said with a yawn and a stretch. "Good night then."

"Good night," said Jorey.

In the morning, Jorey and Timmy were up first. Porto was snoring like a piglet and rubbing his swollen belly. They decided to let him sleep and walked into the kitchen.

"Good morning, boys." Jorey's Mom was in her usual good mood. She was scrubbing the floor in yellow rubber gloves that reached all the way past her elbows. She was wearing her cleaning overalls, covered by an apron that was filled with every cleaning utensil and solution known to man. "I've set out a plate of eggs for each of you." She pointed to a plate full of eggs. "That one is for Jaden."

Suddenly the phone rang. She walked into the other room to answer it, dusting along the way.

"Hurry! Dump on the garlic while your mom's gone!"

Jorey dug through the spice cabinet, and pulled out the garlic shaker.

"Hurry! Hurry!"

"I am. I am. There, that should be enough." He had dumped so much garlic that you could barely see the eggs underneath. Just as he put the shaker back, his mom, Jaden, and Porto walked in.

Jaden sat down in front of his plate and picked up his fork.

"Jaden, Mrs. Gooseberry called. She asked if you could walk her dog early."

"Thanks, Mom. Here, Porto." Jaden slid his plate in front of Porto. Porto had already inhaled his eggs. "You can have mine. I had better get going."

Porto didn't hesitate. "Thanks, Jaden!" he said, grabbing the plate with wide hungry eyes. He scooped up a giant fork full and shoved it in his mouth. "Yum! These are great!"

Timmy and Jorey put their hands on their foreheads and sighed. Another plan was ruined, pulverized, demolished, and down the drain.

After breakfast, Jorey and Timmy explained their plan to Porto.

"That's why they tasted so good. I love garlic! Do you guys have any other ideas?"

"No," said Jorey.

"Me neither," said Timmy. "I think the only thing you can do now is tell your parents."

"No! Not yet," Jorey said. "There's got to be something we can do."

"I think we should try shaving him again," said Timmy. "This time, we will do it right."

"Maybe you're right," Jorey said. "Maybe you two better call your parents to see if you can stay the night again."

Timmy and Porto went in the other room to call, leaving Jorey alone to think. What was he going to do? Jaden was his big brother, someone he loved more than anything. He couldn't just leave him to this horrible fate. If their roles were reversed, Jorey was sure Jaden would do something for him.

He looked up just in time to see Jaden walk in to his room.

"Hey, Jorey. What's up?" Jaden plopped himself on the bed and started rubbing his leg.

"Does your bite still hurt?"

Jaden tore off his bandage to reveal a swollen red ankle with four small holes. "Yeah, it still hurts, but it will be all right."

Jorey wiped a tear from his eye.

"What's wrong?" Jaden asked, placing a hand on Jorey's shoulder.

Jorey jumped. "I just got something in my eye—that's all."

"Well, if you need anything, just ask." Jaden stood up to leave. "I wouldn't want anything to happen to my favorite little brother." He ruffled Jorey's hair, and left the room.

Jorey's heart sank. He felt worse than ever—he just had to find a way to help his brother.

Timmy and Porto walked into Jorey's room acting excited as ever.

"We can stay!" they said.

"That's good—but the only thing I can think of is to try to shave him again."

"That sounds fun!" Porto said through a mouthful of candy. "I didn't get to go last time."

Timmy slugged him in the shoulder. "That's because you fell asleep!"

"I couldn't help it. Turkey puts me to sleep, so does pizza and lasagna and corn dogs and—"

"Okay, okay!" said Timmy. "We get it; almost anything puts you to sleep!"

"Come on guys," Jorey said. "Let's plan how we're going to shave Jaden tonight. I don't want any mistakes this time."

Timmy said, "I don't think we should use shaving cream this time."

"Agreed." said Jorey.

"Why?" asked Porto.

Jorey and Timmy explained what had happened—and then they planned a new strategy.

Chapter Eight

After making their plan, the friends found Jorey's old black joggers, black pajamas, a black shirt, and a pair of black pants.

"There," said Jorey after they had all changed their clothes, "it will be hard to see us in the dark now."

"I feel stupid," Porto said. Jorey's joggers were way too small for him. They were tight all over, and his belly poked out like a beach ball stuffed in a sock.

"You look fine," Timmy said. "I'm the one that looks stupid." Jorey's pajamas were way too big for him. His arms only came halfway down the sleeves—and the pants dragged a foot behind him on the floor.

"You both look fine," Jorey said. "Besides we have to wear black in case Jaden wakes up."

The boys played games, told jokes, and talked until Jaden walked into his room. All three of them put their ears to the wall.

"You guys think this will work?" asked Porto.

"Think what will work?" a voice said behind them.

They turned around and flattened themselves against the wall. Jaden was standing in Jorey's doorway. All three boys froze.

"What are you guys doing?" Jaden asked, stepping into the room.

The boys slid across the wall, farther from Jaden.

Finally Jorey said, "We were listening for bugs . . . bugs in the wall."

Jaden tilted his head. "What makes you think we have bugs in the wall?"

"Um . . . we heard in school that sometimes you can hear bugs in the wall by putting your ear against the wall."

Jaden placed his ear against the wall. "I don't hear anything."

"Great. I guess we don't have any bugs," Jorey said.

Jaden shook his head. "You guys are funny. I'd like to stay and help you listen for bugs, but I've got to lie down. My legs hurt." He rubbed he legs. "Dad says its growing pains. Good night."

"That was close," Timmy said.

"Did you guys hear what Jaden said? Turning into a werewolf is staring to hurt. Come on guys—we've got to find a way to stop him from changing into a werewolf."

"I know!" said Timmy. "If shaving him don't work, we can put the silverware back!"

"We don't want to hurt him," Jorey said.

"It might not hurt him," Timmy said. "It just might chase the werewolf out of him."

Jorey said, "I guess it's worth a try—anything is better than nothing."

They listened at the wall until they heard Jaden snoring.

"All right guys," Jorey said. "Let's do it."

They tiptoed into Jaden's room. This time, they left the shaving cream and brought a flashlight. When they were at Jaden's bed, Jorey stopped them.

"Timmy, you hold the flashlight. Porto, you watch and see if he wakes up—and I'll shave him." Timmy and Porto nodded—even though no one could see them in the dark. Jorey flipped on the razor. Jaden moved a little when he heard the sound, but stayed asleep. Jorey slowly placed the razor on what felt like Jaden's upper lip. He couldn't see very well because Timmy was shaking so badly that he kept moving the light.

"Okay," Jorey whispered. "I think I got it—now we need to do under his arms." He motioned for Porto to lift up Jaden's arms. As Porto lifted, Jaden snorted and turned, but stayed asleep. In a few moments, Jorey was done. "Okay" he whispered. "Let's go."

They tiptoed back to Jorey's room.

"We did it!" Porto shouted. Jorey and Timmy covered Porto's mouth and shushed him.

"We don't want to wake Jaden up!" Jorey whispered.

It was too late; Jaden was already heading down the hall to the bathroom.

"Hurry!" Jorey said. "Lie down and pretend you're asleep."

They dove for their covers and started to snore. Jaden stumbled into the bathroom and turned on the light.

All was quiet—until a loud scream cracked into a bloodcurdling howl.

"What happened to my mustache?"

The boys waited and waited; it was so quiet they could hear themselves breathing—and their hearts beating. Suddenly there was a sound of a wrapper being opened in the dark.

"Porto! Now's not the time to be eating!"

"Sorry. I get hungry when I'm nervous."

Jaden walked into Jorey's room. "Hey," he whispered. "You guys awake?" Nobody moved, or said a word. "Hey, guys."

When nobody answered, he went back to his room.

"That was close," Timmy said.

"Too close," Jorey said. "What do you think, Porto?"

The only answer was a snore. Porto had fallen asleep with a half-eaten caramel bar hanging out of his mouth.

Chapter Nine

In the morning, the boys didn't know if Jaden knew what they had done—or if he thought it was something he had done in his sleep.

They walked into the kitchen and froze with surprise. Jaden was sitting at the table with only half a mustache.

"Did you sleep well?" Jaden asked.

Nobody said a word—they just stared at him.

After a moment, Jorey said, "Um, good morning, Jaden."

"Um, yeah," said Timmy. "We slept soundly all night."

"Slept like a log," Porto added.

Jaden rubbed his upper lip. "I wish I had. I think I walked in my sleep again and shaved off half my mustache. It was just starting to come in good too."

The boys looked at each other, but none of them knew what to say.

"You kids ready to eat breakfast?" Jorey's mom set a plate of pancakes on the table. "They're fresh and hot."

"Thanks, Mom," Jaden said as he took a pancake and placed it on his plate. "They smell good."

While she wasn't looking, the boys quickly put the silverware back in the drawer and raced back to the table. Jorey lost again—and ended up sitting next to Jaden.

When she went to the drawer to get the plastic forks, she opened it and stared in amazement. "Isn't that just the strangest thing?"

"What's that, Mom?" Jaden asked.

"Well," she said, still staring into the drawer. "Last night I disinfected the drawers with vinegar, bleach, abrasive scrub, and your dad's power washer. All that I put in this one was plastic forks, but now my silverware is back. Oh well." She placed the silverware on the table. "Eat up, boys—I've got work to do."

Jaden picked up a fork and bit a pancake. "Ouch!"

The friends looked at each other and nodded.

"What happened, honey bun?" his mom asked.

"I bit my tongue."

Jorey, Timmy, and Porto each grabbed a pancake and ran for Jorey's room.

The friends ate their pancakes in Jorey's room.

"I told you he was a werewolf," Jorey said.

Timmy and Porto nodded.

"Yep!" Timmy said. "The silver hurt him all right."

"He said he bit his tongue," Jorey said, shaking his head.

"That's because his teeth are growing too," Timmy said, "and the silver hurt him."

"What do we do now?" asked Porto.

"I don't know," Jorey said. "But we have got to do something. I don't want Jaden to be a werewolf! I think the only thing left to do is tell my dad"

"If that's what you have to do," Timmy said. "Wish me luck." Jorey pulled on his pants and left the room.

He found his dad reading a book on the couch.

"Dad, we need to talk."

"About what, buddy?"

His mom came in with two glasses of chocolate milk. "Here you go, boys. I thought you might like a drink. I'll take some to your friends too."

"Dad, I've got some awful news." Jorey took a big gulp of milk. "It's about Jaden."

"Is something wrong?"

"Oh yeah!" Jorey took another gulp of milk. He knew the best thing to do was to tell him straight out. "Jaden is growing hair under his arms and on his face." Jorey knew his dad had read books about werewolves, so he was expecting him to look surprised, shocked, or even amazed. Instead, he smiled.

"It's okay, buddy. I know."

"You know?"

"Don't worry, buddy. We all go through these changes in our bodies. It happens to all the men in our family around Jaden's age. It's natural."

Jorey spat his milk all over the couch. "It's natural!"

What if it wasn't the dog bite after all? What if was just like in *The Werewolves of Old*? That would mean that his normal, loving, helpless, poor, poor, family comes from a long, long, line of evil-eyed, flesh-eating, fang-bearing, claw-wearing, ratty-haired, tick-flea-ridden, terrible werewolves!

He took another gulp of milk.

"Yep, son—and in a few more years, you'll go through the same thing."

Jorey choked, causing chocolate milk to explode out of his nose!

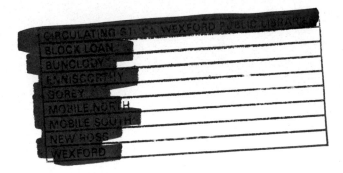

CPSIA information can be obtained
at www.ICGtesting.com
Printed in the USA
LVOW04s1459200416

484522LV00015B/528/P

9 781466 948686